The CAT *in*/*the* MANGER
Wilbert Longtail's Christmas

STEVE VASSEY

Illustrated & Designed by Anthony Hightower

Contents

Dedication

In memory of the real Wilbert Longtail, a truly special cat.

Chapter 1

Wilbert Longtail

"Here, kitty kitty kitty! Here, kitty kitty!" Anna's familiar, little-girl voice roused Wilbert Longtail from his nap in the warm bed of pine straw under Mr. Rucker's azalea bushes.

Wilbert turned one ear toward the sound. He stuck his front legs out in a long, leisurely stretch and yawned a wide yawn. Then he arched his back and stood on tiptoes to stretch the rest of his orangey-red striped body. As he did, his tail curled around and under until it made a perfect "O" behind him.

"Here, kitty kitty!" Anna called again.

"Mmm," Wilbert said to himself. "Must be supper time." He yawned once more and scratched an itch behind his left ear. Then he raised his tail straight in the air and started home.

Wilbert spied his five-year-old human waiting on the front steps. As his head poked from behind the bushes Anna stamped her foot and called again, "Hurry up, Wilbert. It's cold!"

Wilbert scampered across the worn paved road and around the big pine tree in the front yard. He curled around Anna's leg a few times and tickled her knees with the white tip of his tail. "Meow-yow-yow," he said, which is cat-talk for: "Okay, let's eat!"

Anna scooped Wilbert up and cuddled him against her. Since she'd found him beside the old tool shed next to the schoolyard, he'd grown into a very large cat with very long tail.

"He'll grow into it," the vet had told Daddy on their first visit. But Wilbert's tail had more than kept pace with the rest of him.

Anna's older brother, Ryan, named him Wilbert, after his youth baseball team, the Wilbert Warriors. Daddy had added Longtail because: "A proper cat has to have a proper last name."

Wilbert put a paw on each of Anna's shoulders and nuzzled his nose against her neck. Anna's long, strawberry blonde curls swirled around him until it was hard to tell where cat stopped and little girl started.

Anna scratched Wilbert under the chin and behind his ears. Then she rubbed the back of his neck and the top of his head. Wilbert felt a warm glow inside and let out a long *ththtttt*.

Anna smiled as Wilbert's *ththtttt* tickled her ear. "Poor kitty," Anna said, "you still haven't learned to purr, have you?"

Wilbert let out another *ththtttt*. It was true. No matter how hard he tried, he couldn't purr. All he could manage was a whispery *ththtttt*.

Scooter, the old Siamese cat that lived with the family, purred so loudly Wilbert could hear him from the other end of the house. Wilbert loved to listen to Scooter purr. The sound always made him happy.

He'd asked Scooter one day if he'd please show him how. But Scooter only scratched his chin and said, "Wish

I could, son. Truth is, I don't know how I do it. When I'm happy, this rumble starts deep down in my throat and comes out as a purr. The happier I get, the louder I purr. Sorry I can't explain any better. It's just a thing cats do."

"Every cat but me," Wilbert said with a sigh.

Anna carried Wilbert into the living room. He lifted his nose and sniffed the air. Something smelled strange. He peered over Anna's shoulder. There, in the middle of the room was, of all things, a tree. What's a tree doing inside the house? Wilbert wondered. Trees are outside things.

Anna lifted him up to the small fir. "Look, Wilbert! Daddy got us a *real* tree for Christmas this year. Doesn't it smell wonderful?"

He sniffed a few times more. Smells like a tree, Wilbert thought. What's so special about that?

Wilbert wiggled in Anna's arms until she set him down. He left her with the tree and strolled into the kitchen for his supper.

He crunched the star-shaped bits Mama poured for him and sampled a taste of the moist, canned food Scooter ate. Then he washed his face and paws before going back into the living room to study the tree Anna was so excited about.

The orangey-red cat stopped in amazement. While he'd been eating, Daddy had wrapped long strings of tiny, bright lights around and around the tree until it twinkled like the nighttime sky. Anna, Ryan, and Mama were hanging small shiny balls and other colorful shapes on the branches.

Wilbert walked over and sniffed the newly decorated tree. Another cat looked back at him from one of the shiny balls. He reached a paw toward it.

"Don't get any ideas, Wilbert," Daddy warned. "Christmas trees aren't for cats to play with."

Wilbert backed up a few steps. When Daddy used that particular voice, he knew he'd better be careful. He waited until Daddy turned his attention back to the tree, then quickly swatted the ornament. The silver ball fell to the carpet with a soft tinkle.

"Wilbert, scat!" Daddy said in a loud voice.

Anna scooped Wilbert into her arms before he could get into more mischief. "It's okay if you look, Wilbert, just don't play with the ornaments." She held him up to her shoulder and pointed at the tree. "Look. I put the manger right in the front where everyone can see it."

Nestled in the branches among the twinkling lights was a small, wooden building. It reminded Wilbert of the storage shed where he was born. Inside, a man and a woman knelt by a bed of straw, just like Wilbert's pine straw bed under Mr. Rucker's azaleas. Lying in the bed was a small human *kitten*.

Two other humans stood to the side, holding long sticks. Different kinds of animals lay behind them. Wilbert recognized the cow from the time he'd gone to Grandmama's with Ryan and Anna. But he had no idea *what* the other animals were, especially the one with the huge hump on his back. That looked extremely uncomfortable.

Wilbert hopped down from Anna's arms and sat by the couch, watching the humans decorate the tree. He tilted his head to one side and twitched the white tip of his tail. It's nice, Wilbert thought, but I still don't see what all of the fuss is about. So, as cats usually do when they need time to think, Wilbert found a cozy spot next to the heater vent and curled his long tail around him for an evening nap.

Chapter 2

The Stable

Wilbert woke, sticking out his front legs in a long, lei-surely stretch. He stood on tiptoes and arched his back to stretch the rest of him, while his long tail curled around and under into a perfect "O." He opened his mouth and curled his tongue in a wide yawn. In the middle of his stretch, a huge, wet nose bumped him end over end onto the hard, dirt floor.

"Phft-hisss!" Wilbert spat, his tail bristling like a bot-tlebrush. "Who hit me? What's going on?"

The face of a brown cow gazed down at him. "Sorry," she said in a deep, mellow voice. "I was hungry and you were sleeping in my dinner. So I just nosed you out of the way."

"Oh," Wilbert said, his tail slowly returning to normal. "I'm sorry. I didn't realize…" Wait a minute. What was a cow doing in the living room? Wilbert shook his head and looked around. This wasn't the living room! Where were Anna or Ryan—or the Christmas tree?

He sniffed. The air smelled like dry grass and dust and animals. He turned his head and looked around again. He was in a large room with a dirt floor. The low roof rested on rough, wooden beams. Off to one side were other ani-mals: a funny, gray creature with long ears, and a strange, tan-colored beast with a large hump on its back—just like the ones Anna had shown him in the manger on the Christmas tree. Only the humped animal was huge, taller than the cow that had bumped him out of her dinner.

"Where am I?" Wilbert asked the cow, who calmly chewed her hay. "How did I get here?"

"Oh, dear," the cow said. "I may have bumped you harder than I meant to. Don't worry. I'm sure you'll be all right."

She gathered another mouthful of straw. "You're in a stable where the humans keep their animals at night. You were asleep when I came in earlier this evening."

"But I live with my humans in the house next to the big pine tree," Wilbert said, shaking his head. "I don't know *how* I ended up in your food."

A shuffling noise drew Wilbert's attention to two humans in the far corner of the stable. One of them, a man, gathered straw into a thick pile. The other, a woman, leaned against the wall holding her hands against her middle.

The man took off a long, funny-looking, coat and spread it over the straw. As he helped the woman lie down on the makeshift bed, Wilbert noticed her large tummy. It was bigger than his had gotten the time he ate a whole piece of chicken Mama gave him

"What's wrong with her?" Wilbert asked.

"She's about to give birth," the cow said, still chewing.

"You mean she's having kittens?"

The cow chuckled a low, moo-like laugh and shook her head. "No, she's having a baby—a small human, just like a kitten is a little cat. Humans usually have only one."

"Oh." Wilbert sat watching the humans, his head tilted

to one side, the white tip of his tail wiggling slowly back and forth. After a long while, he roused himself from his thoughts. "Well, I suppose I should find out where I am if I want to get back to Anna and Ryan," he said to no one in particular. With a flick of his tail, he walked over to the gray animal with the long ears.

Wilbert crouched down beside the stall where the long-eared animal was eating grain and straw from a small trough. With a graceful leap, he sprang quietly to the top of the stall's railing so he would be eye-to-eye with the creature.

"Excuse me," Wilbert said in his most polite tone. "Would you tell me what kind of animal you are? I've never seen such impressive ears on anything other than a rabbit. And you're obviously *not* a rabbit."

"Why, thank you," the gray animal replied in a singsong voice. "They *are* marvelous ears, aren't they? I'm quite proud of them." He dipped his head toward the cat. "I'm a donkey."

"Do you live in this stable?" Wilbert asked. "I'm not sure how I got here. I was hoping you could tell me."

"No, I only arrived a short while ago." He pointed his nose toward the humans in the far corner. "I carried the woman on my back from far away. I'm resting here until I'm needed again."

"Thank you. Enjoy your dinner and rest." Wilbert hopped from the wall. "Maybe the large animal with the hump on his back can help me."

The donkey nodded and returned to his grain and straw. "Be careful," he said around a mouthful of food. "Camels can be ornery creatures—and they're always arrogant."

"Camel," Wilbert said under his breath. "So *that's* what he is."

He padded across the dirt floor to where the tan animal lay chewing his cud. "Hello," he said, looking at the camel's face high above him. "Do you live in this stable?"

The camel looked down his long nose at the orang-ey-red cat. He shook the tassels on his harness and snorted. "I do *not*. I carried my master across the desert for many days to get here. *My* home is far away."

"Is your master one of the humans resting on the straw in the corner?" Wilbert lifted his paw toward the man and woman.

"Indeed not." The camel sniffed. He curled his lips around in a funny way and looked at Wilbert as if he'd smelled something awful. "*My* master wears silk cloth and gold rings, not dirty traveling clothes like those two. He's staying at the inn."

Wilbert settled back on his hindquarters. "What's an inn?"

"Don't you know *anything*, cat?" the camel drawled. "An inn is like a stable where humans stay. They have rooms with beds in them."

"Then why aren't those two staying at the inn?" Wilbert

asked.

"There are probably no rooms left, especially for the likes of them. This place is overrun with humans. I've never seen so many in one place before. It's a wonder we animals have a place to sleep tonight."

Wilbert had a thought. "My human has a small decoration on her Christmas tree that she called a manger. It looks a lot like this place. Do you know if this is a manger?"

The camel chewed for a minute in thought. "I've traveled to many places, but I've never heard of a tree called Christmas. I *have* heard the word, manger, though. That's what some humans I once met called the feed troughs, but this is definitely a stable."

Wilbert's cat curiosity got the better of him. Before he could think better of it, he posed another question to the large tan animal: "I've never seen a camel before. Is that hump on your back uncomfortable?"

The camel leapt to his feet, the tassels on his harness lashing about. "Ignorant cat! How *dare* you insult my hump? Why, it's one of the finest to be found on the back of a camel. Go away. I've had enough of your questions."

Before Wilbert could say, "Cat," the animal drew back his head and squirted a long stream of spit right at his head.

The cat jumped as quickly as he could, but the spit landed squarely on his back. He ducked under the cow's feed trough in case the camel sent any more his way.

"Hee, hee, hee haw!" the donkey laughed, as Wilbert scampered for cover. "I *told* you to be careful."

Wilbert cleaned the sticky mess from his fur. "You were right," he said as he licked his back. "Camels can be *very* ornery. I only asked a simple question…"

The woman in the corner suddenly cried out. Wilbert jumped at the noise and bumped his head on the bottom of the trough. "Ouch," fussed the orangey-red cat, rubbing his head with his paw. "What's going on?"

"The woman is beginning to give birth," the cow rumbled.

"Why does she cry out like that?" Wilbert asked.

"There is great pain in giving birth," the cow replied. "She cries out to ease the worst of it."

Wilbert turned to watch the two humans, utterly spellbound. He'd never seen a birth before. Slowly, he crept closer, until he sat not an arm's length from the woman. His head leaned curiously to one side and the white tip of his long, striped tail twitched.

The woman lay back to rest for a moment and noticed him sitting nearby. "A cat! Oh, shoo it away, Joseph. Mother said cats will smother babies."

The man touched her shoulder and spoke softly. "You lie back and rest. You shouldn't believe every old wives' tale you hear." He smoothed the damp hair from the woman's forehead. "Be glad the cat is here. I'm sure this old stable has its share of rats. He'll keep them away from our baby. I'd much prefer him to an old rat, wouldn't you?"

Wilbert studied the man called Joseph. He had a kind face and a short beard that made Wilbert think of Daddy.

Daddy! The thought reminded him of home. He heaved a long sigh. I still don't know how to get back—or how I got into this stable.

He walked over to an empty stall near the two humans and hopped up into the feed trough. He curled himself tightly into one corner and rested his head on his front paws so he could watch the humans without troubling the young woman.

Home, the orangey-red cat thought. I wonder if I'll ever see Anna and Ryan again. He felt as lost as he had as a kitten by the old shed so long ago.

He lay quietly, as thoughts of home danced through his mind. Slowly, his eyelids lowered, until he was fast asleep, his long tail curled around him.

Chapter 3

The Baby and the Shepherds

Wilbert awoke with a start. Brilliant, golden light filled the stable, reaching into every nook and corner. He shook his head and sniffed. A warm, wet smell hung in the air. He turned to ask the cow what was happening when the evening was split with a shrill *waaaaah, waaaaaaah!*

"A son!" Joseph shouted with joy. "Praise God! A fine, healthy boy, just as we were promised!"

Wilbert peeked over the edge of the trough. The man held a naked baby high in the air and danced with happiness. The golden light shone brighter, and the room filled with the most marvelous music Wilbert had ever heard, like thousands of humans singing together. He looked around in surprise. Where was the sound coming from? The man and the woman were the only humans in sight.

Joseph cuddled the baby to his chest. As the brilliant light faded and the music dimmed, he wrapped the infant in clean cloths from his travel pack. Then he kissed the child on the forehead and laid him in his mother's arms. "A fine son indeed." The father smiled down at them. "Both of you rest. It's been a long day, but one with a blessed ending."

Wilbert walked over to where the mother and baby lay on the straw bed. Gently, he brushed his nose against the woman's arm and gazed up at her face. "Meowrrrup?" he asked quietly.

The woman smiled at him. "Well, hello again, cat," she said in a quiet, tired voice. "Have you come to see our baby?"

Wilbert pawed softly at the woman's arm.

"My husband says I shouldn't fear your presence. You're our guardian from the rats that haunt the stable. So here, my brave protector, it's my pleasure to show you my son."

She pulled the cloth away from the baby's face and held him up for Wilbert to see. "His name," the woman said proudly, "is Jesus."

Wilbert peered into the face of the newborn, wrinkling his nose at the unfamiliar smell. It was a fine baby, at least as far as he could tell. The infant smiled, and Wilbert grew warm and happy inside. A whispery *ththtttt* sounded unexpectedly from his throat. Yes, he thought, this is a *very* fine baby.

"Joseph," the woman called, "I need to sleep now, but I've nowhere to lay the child. I can't just put him on this pile of straw. If only we'd been able to bring the wonderful cradle you made."

Joseph rose from where he sat nearby. "I'll see what I can find, Mary." Glancing around the room, his eyes fell on a large, unused feed trough nearby. "This will do nicely, I think." Joseph piled the inside thickly with fresh straw. Then he folded another of the long, coat-like garments several times to make a mattress for the child. Pulling the makeshift bed over to his wife, Joseph gently took the baby from her arms and laid him in the soft folds of cloth. "There," he said, "a cradle fit for a king."

Mary ran her fingertips over cradle. "Yes, it is." She laid her hand gently on her child, closed her eyes, and drifted off to sleep.

Wilbert considered curling up in the straw at Mary's feet when a rumble in his middle reminded him he hadn't eaten in a long while. He prowled around the room and peeked in every stall, but he couldn't find a food bowl anywhere.

He warily eyed the sleeping camel. He wasn't about to ask that ornery creature anything. Instead, he padded over to the donkey's stall. "Do you know where the bowl is with my food in it?"

The donkey turned his long ears toward the cat. "All I've seen is grain and straw. If you can eat that, you're welcome to some of mine."

Wilbert sniffed the donkey's trough. It smelled like the flowerbed around the pine tree back home. "Thanks," he said, "but I don't think I can."

"Suit yourself," the donkey said. "It's all I have to offer."

Wilbert nosed around the stable a while longer, but found nothing other than more straw and grain. The hungry cat was just about to walk outside when the door opened and a group of smiling faces peered in.

"Phft-hisss!" Wilbert spat, jumping back from the sudden appearance of the humans. They smelled like the old wool sweater Anna let him sleep on. Each carried a long stick with its end bent into a large hook.

"*Shalom aleichem,*" one of the group said to Joseph. "We

were with our flock in the nearby fields, when the night exploded with light and the most wonderful music. The sky above us filled with angels, more than could be counted. They sang praises and told us a child had been born, here in a stable, who would be a savior to our people."

Wilbert pondered the man's words. Was this the same light and wonderful music he'd heard? But he'd seen no angels, whatever they were. And what was a savior?

"We've searched the town and were finally led to this place," another of the men said. "This must be the babe the angels spoke of."

"We see your wife is sleeping," a third said. "But may we see the child who'll be our king?"

Aleichem shalom. Welcome, shepherds." Joseph motioned them inside. He bent down to Mary, gently waking her, and spoke quietly into her ear. She nodded to the group of eagerly waiting men and reached into the makeshift cradle to hold her son before them.

One by one, the men knelt before Mary and the baby. They bowed their heads and said quiet words Wilbert couldn't hear. They must have been nice words, though, because both Mary and Joseph beamed until their faces shone. Then, as suddenly as they'd arrived, the shepherds left through the open door.

The men's laughter drifted back through the stable. Then Wilbert heard their voices lift in song as they faded into the night.

How odd, he thought.

Chapter 4

Wilbert Goes Exploring

The gurgle in Wilbert's stomach turned into a noisy growl. He was hungry. Maybe I can find something to eat outside, he thought. He jumped from the trough and padded through the stable door.

"What a strange place," he said as he stepped from the stable. Only the light of a few lanterns hung by doorways broke the darkness. The streets were dusty, hard dirt. And there wasn't a car to be seen, only a few people and the occasional animal, clopping along behind its master.

He turned down a narrow alley. At its end, he found a bit of meat in a battered metal plate beside the back door of a building. He carefully looked around for anything dangerous, then settled on his haunches to chew at the morsels.

He'd just swallowed the first bite when the night erupted in vicious barks. "Hey, cat! Get away from my food," a large, grizzly, brown dog growled. "Why, I ought to bite your tail off. In fact, I think I will." He lunged at the cat, teeth bared.

Wilbert danced up on his toes. His spine arched and the hairs on his back and tail stood on end, making him look larger than he already was. "Phft-hisss!" Wilbert warned. He raised one paw and exposed the sharp, shiny claws that hid beneath his soft fur. "Stay back, dog! I was only trying to find some supper. Come any closer, and I'll put a dozen scratches on your nose."

Startled, the big dog skidded to a stop—exactly what Wilbert wanted. Before the dog could reconsider, Wilbert grabbed a mouthful of food and darted back up the alley. The door of a nearby building hung partly open. He slipped inside.

He paused in the dark interior to catch his breath. "Whew!" he gasped, dropping his mouthful of food on the ground. "That was close! I wouldn't have made two bites for that nasty creature. If he hadn't paused at my warning, I might've been *his* dinner tonight."

Wilbert twitched his right ear toward a *scritch-scritch* in the corner of the room. Slowly, carefully, he raised his head and turned to the noise. Two mice scratched through a bag of spilled grain. His stomach gurgled at the sight of a potential meal. Wilbert sank down close to the floor and tensed the muscles in his legs. His tail jerked in quiet little twitches, sweeping the dusty floor behind him.

He waited until just the right moment when both mice were looking away, his body poised to move in a split second. Quick as a blink and silent as a thought, Wilbert leapt. The two mice darted into the shadows, barely escaping his paws.

Wilbert watched the mice scurry into the dark recesses of the room. It was just as well, he thought with a sigh. Anna didn't like for him to hunt. In fact, she'd once scolded him when he proudly brought her a blue jay and laid it on the front steps. Most of the time, he just play-hunted. He'd hide in the azaleas and watch the squirrels scampering around the big pine tree. Then, with a huge leap and a twitch of his long tail, he'd chase them up into the branches. It was great fun. Wilbert would sit there being so very proud, while the squirrels chattered angrily above him.

Wilbert ate the bits of meat he'd gotten from the dog's bowl. There wasn't much, but it would have to do. He washed his face and paws and, with the growl in his stomach quieted, he returned to the stable. He was careful to stay far away from the building where the big dog lay sleeping by the back door.

A single lantern lit the stable with a soft, yellow glow. Mary, Joseph, and the baby slept in their corner of the room. The other animals quietly dozed in their stalls, except for the arrogant camel, who chewed noisily in his sleep.

Wilbert found a soft spot in the straw near Mary's feet and walked around on it a few times to make a cozy little nest. He hoped Anna wouldn't mind if he wasn't curled up on the foot of her bed tonight. He still had no idea how to get home. So many things had happened; he hadn't begun to find his way back.

Wilbert settled into the straw and curled his long tail around him. He rested his head on his front paws and let his eyelids close halfway. "Maybe I'll find my way home tomorrow," he said to no one in particular. "Maybe someone will show me the way." The orangey-red cat with the long, striped tail closed his eyes and thought about Anna and the house by the big pine tree.

Chapter 5

Wilbert and the Rat

Wilbert was drifting off to sleep, thinking pleasant thoughts of Anna, Ryan, Mama, and Daddy, when a soft scuffle from the far corner of the stable turned his ears in that direction. "Babies," a quiet voice hissed from behind the grain sacks. "I smell newborn babies. Who wants dusty old grain when there's a soft, pink baby nearby?"

Wilbert kept very still. He cracked one eyelid and peered across the stable.

"Maybe I'll nibble a tender, little ear or bite a tasty, little toe," the slippery voice continued. "Oh, what a delight has been brought to me tonight."

Wilbert shivered at the malicious words. He opened both eyes to watch the corner. Carefully, he shifted his feet underneath his body. The strong muscles in his legs grew taut; his tail twitched beneath the hay.

A slender, wicked-looking head appeared from behind the grain sacks. Two beady, red eyes winked in the lantern light. Small, clawed feet pulled a fat, gray body over the sacks. A hairless pink tail dragged behind.

"A rat," Wilbert murmured. But he sensed this was no ordinary rat. This one had lived in the stable, stealing and eating the animals' grain, until he was nearly the size of Wilbert—and Wilbert was a large cat.

The rat scrambled over the sacks and made his way around the wall toward the baby. His claws made tiny scratching sounds as he moved through the stalls and around the slumbering cow. He paused beside the sleeping humans, his eyes gleaming with delight. "Oh, what a fine treat for myself," the rat whispered. He licked a black tongue over long, white teeth and rubbed his paws over his thin face in eagerness.

Joseph said rats would hurt the baby, Wilbert thought. Mary expects me to protect them. But this rat is so big... He straightened himself in the direction of the approaching creature, sinking down into the straw to hide from the rat's red eyes. His claws dug into the dirt floor of the stable, anchoring him for the leap that would propel him forward.

The rat scrambled up the leg of the trough where the baby lay asleep. He stared at the child for a moment, licking his muzzle, and then reached a paw toward the infant's cheek.

Wilbert hurled himself from the straw, slamming into the rat with all of the power his muscles could give. His claws gripped the fat, gray body and his teeth reached for the slender neck.

But the rat moved quickly. Slippery as fine sand, he slid from Wilbert's grasp. Sharp claws raked the cat's face and the front teeth, like knives, slashed at his shoulder.

Over and over the two animals rolled, teeth and claws flashing. They crashed into the legs of the baby's cradle. The child awoke with a shrill cry.

The two animals separated. Each rolled to a crouch, glaring at the other.

Beyond the rat, Wilbert saw Mary snatch the baby

from the cradle.

"Joseph!" she screamed. "A rat! Wake up!"

Wilbert leapt at the rat again, sending them tumbling across the floor.

He caught glimpses of Joseph grabbing the gnarled stick he'd leaned against the stable wall and raising it in both hands. But Wilbert knew he and the rat were so tangled together, Joseph couldn't strike one without hitting them both. The man stood, watching intently, his stick held ready.

Both animals fought on. Wilbert used every skill he'd ever learned. He clung to the rat with his front claws and kicked with the ones on his back feet. He twisted his head, snapping with powerful jaws at the enemy.

The rat was a practiced fighter. He wriggled and writhed in Wilbert's grasp. His sharp teeth bit at Wilbert's face and body. Claws scratched at Wilbert's face, tearing his nose and cheeks.

Wilbert didn't know how much longer he could fight. The rat showed no sign of slowing or stopping. With his strength nearing its end, Wilbert had a sudden thought. He kicked with his hind legs, shoving the rat away, then slumped to the floor, panting.

The rat squealed a cry of triumph. He raised himself high on his hind legs to plunge down and sink his teeth into the fallen cat.

Wilbert sprang at the rodent. Catching the creature's neck in his mouth, he bit hard, and with a twist of his body, threw the animal against the stable wall. The rat hit with a dull thud and lay still.

Wilbert limped over to examine him. He moved cautiously, in case the animal should attack again. He prodded the body with one paw, alert for any movement, but the rat gave no response. The wicked creature was dead.

With the fight finished, Wilbert realized he hurt all over. Cuts and scratches covered him. Blood matted his orangey-red fur where the rat's teeth had cut a long, ugly gash in his shoulder.

He licked the wound a few times, then turned his head toward Mary. "Meowurrp?" he asked weakly. "Is the baby all right?" Then he collapsed onto the stable floor.

"Joseph," Mary cried. "He's hurt."

It was the last thing Wilbert heard as the room spun into a reddish haze.

Chapter 6

The Messenger

Wilbert opened his eyes and looked around. A bright, golden glow surrounded him. There were no walls or floor, nor ground or sky, only the brilliant radiance. It danced around and through him, becoming a part of him, filling him with the most marvelous feeling.

The orangey-red cat sat up and turned his head to lick the wound on his shoulder. As his rough, pink tongue flicked out, it found only the soft stripes of his fur. Wilbert stared in surprise. Where was the long gash the rat's teeth had made?

Laughter sounded behind him, turning his head. It was musical and beautiful, like bells tinkling or water skipping over rocks in a brook. A sudden smell of roses tickled his nose.

"Your wounds are no more," a gentle voice spoke, still rippling with mirth. "There are no such things in this place."

Wilbert looked for the source of the wondrous sound— and met the gaze of the most beautiful creature he'd ever seen.

He looked like a human man, but shone with a light as bright as the sun. Wilbert started to squint against the brilliance, but realized his eyes didn't hurt at all.

Folds of cloth flowed from the being's shoulders. They shimmered in the golden glow like a rainbow reflected in a scattering of morning dewdrops. A face filled with kindness and love smiled down at him.

"Hello, Wilbert," the beautiful being said.

"Where am I?" the cat whispered.

"You are nowhere—and everywhere." He opened his arms and gestured to their surroundings. "This is a place beyond time. Beyond that, it would be difficult to explain. I must ask you simply to trust me when I say you're exactly where you should be."

"Who are you?" Wilbert asked, somewhat bewildered. "I've never seen any creature as wonderful as you."

The being of light laughed again, and Wilbert heard bells tinkling. "I'm a messenger. You may call me Gabriel.

"That was a brave and selfless thing you did in the stable," he continued. "We are all very proud of you."

"Is the baby all right?" Wilbert asked. "I never found out."

Gabriel gathered the striped cat in his arms. "Even now, you think of the baby first. What a noble creature you are!" He stroked Wilbert's fur, gazing into his eyes. "Yes, the baby is well. Do you realize how special that baby is?"

Wilbert shook his head.

"Well, let me try to explain." The messenger smiled and scratched Wilbert behind his ears. The cat tingled all over at the delicate touch, and a soft *ththtttt* vibrated in his throat.

Gabriel knelt and placed the orangey-red cat in front of

him. "The child you so valiantly protected is a gift—a gift to humans from the One who created all living creatures. He was and is the greatest of gifts.

"In time, the child will bring humans comfort and forgiveness from the things that trouble them. He'll fill their lives with purpose and their hearts with love. He'll show them the pathway home." Gabriel lifted a slender finger. "However, before such a gift can be given, it must be received. That's the choice humans must make.

"The child will grow and teach others. His life will be full of joy and love. He'll do wonderful things; yet he'll also suffer great pain and humiliation, even death." Gabriel's face grew subdued for a moment, then burst into a radiant glow. "But from his suffering will spring a tremendous joy—one so great humankind will celebrate his birth for thousands of years afterward."

Wilbert remembered the baby's gentle smile, and the pleasant way it made him feel. "Does he really have to suffer?"

Gabriel reached down to caress the cat's head. "Yes, Wilbert. For where there is great good, evil will arise to oppose it. You must remember there is purpose to all things, even to the rat you fought. It's often difficult to understand and, at times, seems to make no sense at all. That's when one must accept what's happened and believe a greater purpose is at work."

"But why was I at the stable?" Wilbert asked. "How did I get there? I should've been at home with Anna and Ryan."

With a chuckle, Gabriel tickled the large cat under his chin. "I believe I remember a young cat looking at a Christmas tree and wondering what all of the fuss was about."

Wilbert stared at the messenger, dumbfounded. "You mean Christmas is the celebration of the baby's birth that's lasted for thousands of years?"

Gabriel scooped Wilbert up in his arms again and hugged him with delight. "Yes, my wise friend. *That's* what all the fuss is about."

The messenger paused for a moment, as if in thought. "There is one other thing," he continued. "Such willing sacrifice as you displayed should not go unrewarded. What can I give for so selfless an act?" The beautiful being's mouth pursed, then spread into a dazzling smile. "Ah! I know just the thing."

Gabriel set the cat down and rested one hand gently on Wilbert's head. A warm, tingling happiness spread through his body, even to the tip of his very long tail. "And now, Wilbert, it's time for you to go home. There are two children there who love you very much. Cherish their affection, Wilbert. Not all cats are so fortunate as to receive the love of a human."

Before Wilbert could reply, the messenger faded from sight. The golden light dimmed and the darkness of sleep surrounded the orangey-red cat before he could even curl his tail around him.

Chapter 7

Wilbert's Gift

Wilbert's eyes popped open at the sound of pounding footsteps and Ryan and Anna's excited yells. "It's Christmas!"

Wilbert shook his head and rubbed his eyes with both paws. Home! He was home! But how?

"Look, Ryan." Anna laughed. "Wilbert's asleep under the Christmas tree. I wonder if he saw Santa Claus."

Ryan rolled his eyes and looked at the ceiling. Anna didn't pay him any attention. She pulled the sleepy cat into her arms and hugged him close. "Merry Christmas, Wilbert."

Wilbert poked his nose through the cascade of Anna's strawberry blonde curls and looked around. It was true. He was home again. There were Ryan and Anna, the living room, and the Christmas tree. The manger nestled in the branches right in front of him.

He stared at the small stable for a moment, a flood of memories washing over him. Had it all been just a dream? Then he blinked twice and looked again.

There was the little wooden building, with Mary and Joseph kneeling. There were the donkey, the cow, and the ornery old camel. The shepherds stood to one side, holding their long sticks with the hooks bent on the end. Baby Jesus smiled from his makeshift cradle. And there, asleep beneath the feed trough with his long tail curled around him, was an orangey-red, striped cat.

As Wilbert stared at the scene, he felt a pleasant warmth start deep down inside him. The warmth turned into a tingle, and the tingle into a rumble that rattled loudly in his throat.

"Mama! Daddy!" Anna called to the two sleepyheads who were peeking into the living room. "Listen. Wilbert's purring!"

From his perch on top of the sofa, old Scooter lifted his head at the sound of Wilbert's loud purr. He smiled a cat smile and said, "I knew he could. It was just a matter of time."

Afterward

In case you were wondering, Wilbert Longtail was a real cat, complete with orangey-red stripes and an extraordinarily long tail. He lived with us for five years and, unlike in this story, never did learn to purr beyond a whispery *ththtttt*. Wilbert loved to explore, as all cats do, and was always getting into mischief of one kind or another. Sadly, he disappeared on the night after Halloween in 1994. We like to think he just went on a very long adventure.

~Steve Vassey

Author's Notes

Some who've read the manuscript of Wilbert's adventure have commented on my use of *manger* in referring to the Nativity scene. The word *manger* actually refers to a long open box or trough for horses or cattle—and, I suppose, donkeys and camels—to eat from.

However, when I was growing up, my family always referred to the scene as simply *the manger*. Ours was either set up under the Christmas tree or on the fireplace mantle. In keeping with that small tradition and all its pleasant memories, I've maintained that practice in the story.

You may also be curious why I've not included the three magi. Despite tradition, the three wise men were not present at the Nativity, but arrived afterward. Some speculate their visit may have been as long as two years after Jesus's birth.

The greeting the shepherd gives Joseph, "*Shalom aleichem* (Peace unto you)," and its response, "*Aleichem shalom* (Unto you, peace)," are traditional for the culture and time. It's interesting to note that to not return the greeting was considered acting as a thief, stealing the offered peace.

~**Steve Vassey**

Made in the USA
Lexington, KY
29 September 2017